POWER AND GRACE

THE WORKING HORSE

POWER AND GRACE
THE WORKING HORSE

KLAUS ALVERMANN

PRODUCED BY

CONCEPTS PUBLISHING INC.

CHRONICLE BOOKS · SAN FRANCISCO

To my friends of the Altstadt Café in Mainz.

Author/Photographer: Klaus Alvermann
Art Direction: Dana Jinkins
Editor: Jill Bobrow
Associate Editor: Janet Hubbard-Brown
Production: Bonnie Atwater
Illustrations: Laura Lee

Produced by Concepts Publishing Inc.
P.O. Box 1066
Waitsfield , VT 05673

Printed in Japan.

First Edition

Library of Congress Cataloging-in-Publication Data

Alvermann, Klaus, 1932-
   Power and Grace: the Working Horse/Klaus Alvermann
     p.   cm.
   "Produced by Concepts Publishing Inc."
   ISBN 0-87701-723-9
1. Draft horses.   I. Title.
 SF311.A48 1990
   636.1'5--dc20   89-27969 CIP

Distributed in Canada by
Raincoast Books
112 East 3rd Ave.
Vancouver, B.C.
V5T 1C8
10 9 8 7 6 5 4 3 2 1

Chronicle Books
275 Fifth Street
San Francisco, California 94103

Preface

The following selection of pictures, stories and descriptions of workhorses are the result of my recent travels in the United States and Europe — with me were cameras, books, pots and pans.

After almost twenty years of voyaging around the globe on a small boat with no power other than sails, my return to life on land was greeted by many old friends, including some unexpected ones: on a pasture in Vermont I discovered a group of peacefully grazing horses of distinctly "heavy displacement." As I watched in amazement their slow progress across the field, old memories flooded my thoughts, reminiscences of a time when these horses were still a reality in everyday life — even to the people in a city or town. Today that may seem to be a long time ago!

Whenever someone learns of my recent preoccupation with heavy horses, invariably I am asked the question "why?" But the answer to that still leaves me very much at a loss. Admittedly, my predilection is somewhat unusual.

Growing up in Germany, I spent part of my early childhood in Thuringia on a stud farm which used heavy draft horses for agricultural work. Later, during the post war years when I was back in my home town in a now divided country, I remember the horse-drawn vehicles used for rubble-cleaning and carting goods. Brewery drays were a definite sign of recovery then.

While the sight of a single cart-horse certainly added life to a street in ruins, the lively teams of two were a lot more exciting to watch. Giving the horses a snack would often provide my school-mates and me with an entertaining diversion. For town kids, those friendly draft horses offered one of the rare opportunities to experience physical contact and affection for animals.

Later, the horses slowly disappeared from the scene until the once so familiar sound of iron-clad hooves on cobblestone was not heard any more. And then the cobblestone too became something of the past.

My motivation for 'doing' this book was mainly a wistful one, born out of the desire to bring back to life my vivid memories of our workhorses. The present revival of interest in these horses gave me the unique chance to capture on film a world that seemed irretrievably lost.

However, recently there has been a renaissance of appreciation of workhorses, of their usefulness as well as of their other more subtle values. Plagued by environmental problems some people are looking back into the past to see if some old-fashioned methods may not have been abandoned too hastily — together with some of their heavier four-legged friends.

Horses worked side by side with men and women for thousands of years — and in some small pockets of the world, a few still do. Rediscovering the mystery of this relationship, we may realize that in asserting the survival of the heavy horse we will also be saving a part of ourselves — little as it may seem.

Klaus Alvermann

CONTENTS

Evolution of the Heavy Horse   8
The Belgian
The Percheron
The Shire and the Clydesdale
The Suffolk Punch

Heavy Breeds Today   18

Heavy Horses at Work   48
In the Country
Heavy Horses in Town
Fairs and Competitions
Publicity and Events

Breeding and Rearing   106
Stud Service
Mares and Foals
Pastures and Pastimes
Breaking-In

Farriery   133

Impressions   136
The Amish
Sugaring in Vermont
Sleigh Rides and Logging

EVOLUTION OF THE HEAVY HORSE

The history of the heavy horse is not well documented, nor does it follow a consistent course. It is closely interwoven with the history of humans, encompassing migrations and wars, building and tearing down, growing and harvesting, games and ceremonies — horses took part practically from the beginning.

The earliest documents showing the use of horses date from the Sumerian civilization in the third millennium B.C. These documents depict harnessed horses pulling chariots, but there are no indications of riders! Over a thousand years later one of the first known portrayals of a rider on horseback was carved on an Egyptian relief from the fourteenth century B.C., discovered in the grave of Haremhab.

As strong and beautiful as these early domesticated horses seem to have been, they did not have much in common with the heavy horses of today. Until the middle of the last century oxen were used for heavy work. If horses were used for pulling, it was to take advantage of their speed rather than their power.

One realm, however, where an ox was lucky to be no match to the horse, despite the ox's horns, was on the battlefield. The horse's speed and strength, combined with agility, diligence and courage, led to its importance in battle, and in turn brought about the development of the various heavy breeds. The advent of armored medieval knights and the trend to ever weightier armor and mail encouraged the selection and breeding of a yet stronger and heavier type, the Great Warhorse, a title that seems strange when we look at our "gentle giants" today and misleading when taken out of context of its time. How huge these horses really were we know from their surviving armor of protective leather and metal plating. Their trappings point to horses of rather modest proportions, not surprising as the noble chevaliers who rode them were small by modern standards. They probably would have fallen off their steeds in utter amazement had they been exposed to the sight of a present-day Shire stallion passing through their ranks. Those war horses were nevertheless the forerunners of our heavy horses and thus deserve a closer look.

When Caesar and his Roman soldiers crossed the Alps during the first century B.C. to invade Northern Europe, they found a type of horse most of them had never seen before: a dark, stocky and powerful animal, apparently native to the plains of Flanders but also found along the river Rhine and the Danube. The Romans' descriptions suggest a horse of considerably heavier build than the types common around the Mediterranean such as the Barbs, Arabians or Andalusian horses. It also seems to have been much slower; an abundance of rich pastures diminished the need to be fleet of foot. Marshy lands and a temperate to cold climate are other factors that favored the evolution of this type.

Several hundred years later, in 732 A.D., at the battle of Tours and Poitiers, Charles Martel's heavily armored

men on their sturdy Northern horses stopped the advance of the Muslim armies and their fearsome light cavalries, one of the most fateful victories in Western history. The heavy horse had proven its worth. But the captured stallions of oriental descent made a favorable impression on the French horsemen, and were bred to the heavy European mares in hopes of improved offspring. Thus began more systematic breeding and with additional regions involved, more varieties evolved.

The new breeds shared their distinctive heavy anatomy with the ancient horses of Northern Europe, though they soon surpassed them in size and weight. Perhaps on account of the comparatively cold climate of their habitat the heavy breeds have been labeled "Kaltblut," a term used in German-speaking countries where the word doesn't have the same chilling connotation it may have in English; literally translated the word means "cold-blood," but in horse language this refers to calmness and stolidness. Thoroughbreds and Arabians are "hot bloods," and all other breeds of horses are "warm bloods."

Of the many heavy breeds that evolved over the centuries, approximately two dozen recognized lines exist today, though some are on the verge of extinction. In North America and western Europe, the most popular are the Belgian, Percheron, Shire, Clydesdale and the Suffolk.

Many other breeds of heavy horses exist, often interrelated in one way or another to the horses described here. One of the oldest breeds is the Noriker, a strong and surefooted horse of moderate size from the Austrian mountains. Its history goes back to the times of the Romans and the conquest of the Celtic mountain kingdom of Noricum by Drusus and Tiberius in 16 B.C. Horses of many parts of Europe crossed the region for centuries, contributing to its hardy stock. Charlemagne apparently had a favorable impression of the Norikers when he added the province to his empire. During the Middle Ages the local bishops took an interest in the breeding of these horses; breeders have been guided by their studbooks since the late seventeenth century, something most heavy horse societies would envy.

A good many heavy horses resemble a particular breed, yet cannot be called by that breed's name because they lack a pedigree. They are said to be not of "pure" blood, which seems to be a biased statement if we bear in mind the variety of races in the early ancestry of the pure ones. Those commoners without a family tree are just as close to the heart of the people who look after them. In the enormous amount of work performed by horses over the centuries, the "nameless" breeds are the ones that have borne the main burden.

This book is addressed to the layperson as much as to people who live and work with horses; we see no reason to exclude not-so-pure horses from its pages. After all, were it not for those ordinary ones we wouldn't know the difference — which is often difficult enough for the expert. Distinctions will always be over a horse's head.

9

American Type

European Type

THE BELGIAN

The Belgian, of which there are several varieties, is probably the most typical example of a heavy horse. It has all the general characteristics that distinguish these horses from the lighter breeds, for example, a massive head on a muscular neck, and a heavy, powerful body supported by very substantial legs.

A horse's height is measured at its shoulders, or "withers," and the unit used is called "a hand," which equals four inches or about ten centimeters. The average height of Belgian horses on both sides of the Atlantic is about seventeen hands, the American type being closer to eighteen hands. As with other horses, mares are often slightly smaller than stallions. Though Belgians are not the tallest, they usually are the heaviest (they can weigh over a ton) and are considered by some to be the strongest.

In Europe, "Belgian" is the generic term applied to several slightly differing breeds of heavy horses. There is the old Flemish horse of western Flanders, a region renowned for its heavy horses since the early Middle Ages when they were first imported to England and Scotland to improve the local stock.

Another slightly lighter type, the Ardennes, comes from the hill country between France and Belgium. No other heavy breed was tougher or would subsist on less — virtues that could turn into misfortunes as this horse was much in demand among soldiers, from the Crusaders to Napoleon and through the First World War.

The Brabant is the heaviest of the Belgians and resembles the original type in its purest form. The tradition-conscious Belgian breeders resisted all attempts to introduce fresh blood from other sources, a common practice used to avoid the pitfalls of inbreeding. By all appearances Brabants are none the worse off.

The Belgian horse shows what divergence selective breeding can produce within one breed. The European and American Belgian seem to have little in common apart from their name, origin and a shared history up to the mid-1800s, when Americans began importing them. Americans in the 1860s preferred the Brabant type, particularly the sorrel-colored variety which did not have as much appeal to breeders in Belgium who preferred roans and do up to this day. The contemporary American Belgian is a lighter color than its European ancestors, mostly chestnut with a blond mane and tail. The European Belgian is characterized by its enormous body; American breeders continued striving for a taller horse with more action, a horse that could be used in commercial hitches as well as in agriculture — the result was a splendid horse of slimmer lines and plenty of power.

Publicity and shows played an important role in the development of the American Belgian from the start. Powerful marketing forces were instrumental in dictating taste. The impressive display of Dick Sparrows' forty-horse hitch pulling the Schlitz Circus bandwagon at the famous Fourth of July parade in Milwaukee, Wisconsin, is as much a credit to this breed as are the indefatigable teams of Belgians that can still be seen at work on Amish farms and elsewhere in North America.

Percheron

THE PERCHERON

The Percheron is named after its region of origin, le Perche, a land of rich pastures bordering the valley of the river Huisne in Normandy. The most recognizable feature of the Percheron is its mature color, usually a dappled grey. The color of most Percherons changes as they age. Born black without exception, only a few remain dark; the majority lighten until some turn completely white at a mature age. The traditional dappled rocking horse is a good indication of the breed's widespread appeal. The Percheron's feet show more refinement than those of the other heavy breeds. The average height is sixteen to seventeen hands and their weight can be as much as two thousand pounds. Percherons are known for their particularly friendly disposition.

These were among the first of the heavy horses to arrive in North America; in 1665 Louis XIV had two stallions and a number of mares shipped to Canada. Not until two hundred years later did American buyers start importing the Percheron in a big way. As happened with the Belgian horses, breeders shied away from the more subtly toned colors, favoring the flashier black instead of the greys, as well as a larger size. This predilection almost ruined the breed, at least in French opinion. In order to maintain a lucrative trade, some of the French farmers started crossbreeding their stock with the black Nivernais and other local black breeds. This trend later changed when the boss hostlers of big circus companies discovered the advantages of using the dappled greys for pulling baggage wagons. Not only were they hard to beat for their diligence, stamina and general health, but they were also easier to teach and to match in parades. Considering that the grey horses keep changing color throughout their lives, one might think that trying to match these animals would be difficult. But the consistent irregularity of a dappled horse is easier to match than a more uniformly colored one, especially since the latter may have additional white markings on its head or feet. Some horses' coats fade seasonally as well as with age; this fading is less noticeable with greys. Despite all these small points, there is still a certain preference among North American breeders for the black variety of Percherons.

The Percheron is one of the oldest breeds of draft horses in France. Primarily of North-European stock, its head, neck and feet show a distinctly Arab influence, traits that probably go back to Roman times when Numidian riders passed through Gaul enroute to Britannia. Another source of foreign blood may have been the Arab horses captured in the battle at Tours and Poitiers, not far from the home of the Percherons.

The invention of gunpowder did not completely do away with war horses, including Percherons, as the heavier types were relegated to moving equipment and cannons. When a road system developed in Europe a lighter-colored Percheron variety was favored for stagecoaches, perhaps because of the greater visibility of pale horses at night. Although the railways marked the end of the stagecoach, the heavy teams remained quite a while longer. In Paris and other European cities, teams of Percherons powered the local "bus service."

In North America many Percherons found their way into big teams on farms, where it was not unusual to hitch up thirty or more horses. Even today, the Percheron's friendly and docile temperament makes it the ideal choice for team work. It is not at all rare to see a stallion and a mare working together side by side, unheard of with most other breeds.

Farmers, circus people, trucking companies and breweries of Europe and the New World are not alone in their interest in Percherons. These special horses are also popular in Japan today, where they are used for one-horse sulky races.

Shire

Clydesdale

The Shire and the Clydesdale

Some people may frown at finding the Shire and the Clydesdale described together, especially if they favor one breed more than the other. But since these two breeds are often difficult to differentiate, it is somewhat advantageous to present them side by side.

The Shire's name is derived from the various counties of the English Midlands, such as Yorkshire and Hampshire, where they were first bred. The Clydesdale was developed in Scotland and was named after the river Clyde which flows through Lanarkshire.

Over the years, the Clydesdale seems to have developed more towards the Shire's characteristics rather than vice-versa. Today Shire and Clydesdale share a very distinctive "leggy" look when compared with other draft horses, due to their use as transport horses rather than for agricultural work. They are conspicuous not only for their size. The combination of vivid body colors, white markings, long "feathered" legs with high-stepping gait and a long and lean head held high leaves no doubt that one is looking at a Shire — or a Clydesdale.

It is not as difficult for the expert to see the differences between these horses as it is for normal mortals to recognize subtle differences in conformation or build or movement. Although some say that the Shire is the tallest of the heavy horses, today the two breeds are almost equal in size. The Shire stands seventeen to eighteen hands; the Clydesdale is often the same height, but it may also be shorter. The weights average two thousand pounds. Most Shires are black; they can also be brown, bay or grey. The Clydesdale can be any one of these same colors, but bays are the most common.

Some Clydesdales, however, could never be mistaken for Shires. Shires are never roan, but Clydesdales can be. The real giveaway is the way the white of a Clydesdale's foot will often reach right up to its belly and spread in a mottled fashion, a pattern far less typical for a Shire. The Shire may have no white markings at all, though this would be rare today as four white feet have become the ideal.

When it comes to the head and its white markings — the star or the longer blaze so common on many horses — the Clydesdale shows the least restraint. Occasionally its head may be almost entirely white, at which point the blaze is called a lantern.

One cannot leave this subject without bending down for a closer look at what was referred to above as "feathered" legs, a term for the long, usually white hair covering the horse's legs. When properly groomed, this flowing hair adds the most striking touch to the appearance of a team of Shires or Clydesdales. Although feathering is not uncommon in some other breeds, the trait is not carried to such an extreme, mainly for practical reasons; these adornments can quickly turn into a handicap under severe conditions such as wet soil or frost.

There is almost as much debate about the history of the "Great Horses" of England and Scotland as there is about the subtle differences between them. The lineage of the heavy horses of these two countries follows along parallel lines with many interchanges. Some accounts state that they are the result of crosses between the hardy indigenous pony types (of which the Exmoor pony is probably the best known) and imports of taller, heavier Continental horses thought to be of Flemish and Friesian descent. Other sources indicate that the ancestors of these horses were brought to England in the eleventh century.

Later the Dutch imported their horses to England to help in the work of draining the Fens. It was on such fertile soil that the English created the biggest heavy horse of the time — the Shire. Its original name seems to have been "The Big Black Horse," a generic sounding appellation compared to that of other breeds such as the Clydesdale and the Suffolk who were already known.

The heavy horses in Britain, like those in Europe, were used in warfare as well as for transport and agriculture by the wealthy who could afford their upkeep. Breeding was regulated by various Royal Acts with the purpose of improving size and quality. It is interesting to note that from time to time there were English laws prohibiting the export of heavy horses to Scotland, which indicate that there was an exchange of horses between England and Scotland. This exchange could have affected the purity of either breed. But in the mid-nineteenth century, some outstanding Shires were bought by Scottish breeders and bred with local mares, creating the modern Clydesdale.

The idea of forming breed societies for heavy horses seems to have spread more or less simultaneously throughout the Western horse-farming world during the latter half of the nineteenth and early twentieth centuries — not much of a time span to evaluate the relative purity of any one breed, considering the practice of cross-breeding so common then and the many prior centuries of comparatively uncontrolled breeding. When the Clydesdale Horse Society was founded in 1877, the Clydesdale had been a well-established breed for over half a century. The English followed the Scots' initiative and created a society the very next year, primarily for Shires, but perhaps because of the inherent problems of identifying Shires, they called it the Cart-Horse Society. It was renamed the Shire Horse Society six years later.

Today the Shires and Clydesdales do much of the same work as that of other heavy horses. They were never used in North America for field work due in part to the heavy hair on their legs, but they still can be found at odd jobs in agriculture and forestry. Their main function, however, is ceremonial, in processions and displays. The traditional brewery horse in England is the Shire. Their popularity and advertising value alone more than justify their use.

Suffolk Punch

THE SUFFOLK PUNCH

The Suffolk horse that originated in Suffolk, England is the odd one out among the heavy horses presented in this book. It is generally smaller than the other four breeds, standing fifteen to sixteen hands tall and weighing around sixteen hundred pounds.

The epithet "Punch" implies a particular build, described by some as "barrel-shaped with not much daylight under." The Suffolk stands on clean feet without feather, is evenly colored with few or no markings, and is always "chesnut" (the traditional spelling of the word in Britain when applied to Suffolks). It comes in seven shades: brown-black, dull-dark, light-mealy, red, golden, lemon and bright chestnut.

The Suffolk is the oldest English breed among the island's heavy horses and was recorded by that name as early as the sixteenth century. More accurate descriptions were passed on during the eighteenth century, albeit not very complimentary ones with regard to the horse's aesthetic features — it had a rather big head and a clumsy looking body and legs, a far cry from what the Suffolk is today. Without losing its compact build, the Suffolk has evolved into a horse with a noble head and a shapely body. Its chestnut color, once called sorrel, was established early on in its development.

The question of the Suffolk's origin is not easily answered. A resemblance to Scandinavian heavy horses has led to the assumption that some of its ancestors could have been Nordic. Britain's original horse population consisted mainly of ponies, still reflected in some aspects of the Suffolk's anatomy as well as in its long life, so common amongst ponies. Its longevity — thirty years or more is not the exception — seems to confirm the belief that country living is healthy and adds years to one's life.

The Suffolk has been confined to its home region, East Anglia, during most of its history. It has never had quite the same appeal to overseas buyers as some of the other heavy breeds, though some horses did make it across. There is a loyal and devoted contingent of Suffolk breeders in the United States. Most breeders in other countries were interested in importing the heaviest or tallest horses, as they already had their own lighter breeds; furthermore, the Suffolk was much too ordinary in appearance to excite them. Considering its weight, strength and endurance, the Suffolk is ideally suited to and primarily used for agricultural tasks. Its great width, in front and behind, and short legs give it a low point of draft and enormous pulling power.

Suffolks are noted for their excellent "bottom," or feet, although the opposite used to be true. Once special classifications came into being, breeders kept trying to improve the feet because horse shows started offering prizes for "best feet." Their efforts were so successful that today Suffolks' feet are considered the best among the heavy breeds.

Much of what is known about the more recent history of the Suffolk Punch is owed to the lifework of one man, Herman Biddell. Born in 1832, a farmer and breeder who devoted much of his time to the research of the various lines and strains of the Suffolk, Biddell traveled throughout the countryside visiting numerous farms — and not by automobile! After the Suffolk Horse Society was founded in 1877, Biddell was commissioned to compile the first studbook. His work brought to light a surprising fact: most Suffolk lines of his time led back to a single horse, "Crisp's Horse of Uffort," foaled in 1768. This animal's description differs from its less progenitive contemporaries in that it combined two somewhat incompatible features: the horse was noted for its shapely head and at the same time nobody seems to have bothered to give it a proper Christian name! It must have had everything that mattered, for even today nearly every purebred Suffolk is directly related to this horse.

HEAVY BREEDS TODAY

Heavy horses are often called work horses but routine work has become rare for them. Today, they are used primarily for ceremonial occasions, or, in the case of commercial enterprises such as breweries, these noble creatures are mainly employed for advertising. Since some of the horses no longer make deliveries of beer, there is no need to keep them stabled on brewery premises. Instead, they are kept at farms in the countryside. Some breweries no longer own the horses but lease them from companies specializing in that trade. The horses that were once doing all the carting are now themselves carted off by trailer to their various engagements.

The European Belgian

The European Belgian is the breed most directly linked with the early heavy horses. There are quite a few types, such as the Ardennes and Brabants. Today they are generally referred to under their collective name, Belgians.

Grazing European Belgians in pastures bordering the river Rhine outside Frankfurt.

Belgian brewery teams in Europe.

21

The American Belgian

The American Belgians are often taller and not as heavy as their European ancestors. They are predominately chestnut in color with blond manes and tails.

Above: Whinnying farm horse.
Right: Amish countryside in Ohio.

Above: A team-of-four, plowing a field, upstate New York.
Left: A team in Ohio, hitched up for the grain harvest.
Opposite: A farm horse from the region around Millersburg, Ohio.

Percherons

Of all the heavy horses the Percheron is probably the most lively and dynamic breed, qualities which are further enhanced by a particularly friendly disposition. This breed hails from the Le Perche region in France.

Percherons at the government stud farm, Haras du Pin in Normandy.

The Percheron teams at the Haras du Pin are comprised exclusively of stallions.

The Percheron in America

Originally imported from France, the American Percheron has developed into a less heavy horse of darker colors. All Percherons are born black but many change color; dapples are typical markings on greys.

Left: Lamark, a black American Percheron from Holmes County, Ohio.
Above: A dappled-grey Percheron mare with her foal.
Right: A black and white horse team in the Amish countryside.

Opposite: Grey and solid black Percheron teams working on farms in Ohio.
Below: Towing a canal boat of tourists in the American Midwest.

Clydesdales

Clydesdales and Shires have so many similarities that it might be interesting to compare them. Horse experts might dispute this, based on various measurements of hindquarters or other such characteristics, but the differences will appear inconsequential to the layman. They are among the tallest horses known. There is something youthful about their appearance; similar to young horses or foals, their overall look is dominated by their legs, no doubt on account of the flamboyant coat of "feathers" so typical of them.

This Clydesdale mare has a large white blaze called a lantern. When these white markings extend to the eyes, the pigmentation of the eyes is sometimes affected.

Left: This stallion obviously doesn't get much grooming. Some horses may spend most of the season — if not the entire year — turned out to pasture. Many horse owners feel that an unstabled horse is apt to be healthier than a stabled one.

Above: It is not uncommon to see sheep grazing alongside horses in Scotland.

Right: Three young Clydesdale mares.

Shires

The largest draft horse in England is the Shire, and the most favored ones are black with white feet and a blaze. Another impressive type is the dappled white. Even though you don't often find grey or white Shires, the Whitbread Brewery in London uses them exclusively. Their competitor, Young & Co., uses only black Shires.

Opposite: The white marking or stripe on a horse's head is called a star, and a blaze if longer.

Top: A shire team plowing in Lancashire, England.
Bottom and opposite: Shires are often used as brewery horses.

Suffolk Punch

The Suffolk Punch, the lightest of the heavy horses, has a compact body on comparatively short legs. Its color is always "chesnut."
The Suffolk Punch is an ideal animal for agriculture, efficient at tilling, drilling and many other tasks.

The photographs on these pages were taken at Weylands Farm, Stoke by Nayland, Essex, a farm with a legendary ring to its name that extends well beyond its horizons.

Above: Not everything works without a hitch.
Opposite bottom: When it comes to real work, whether or not the horses are matched doesn't seem to make much difference!

The Comtois, a breed from the Jura, a range of mountains between France and Switzerland, is one of the many heavy breeds not widely known outside Europe. A mountain work horse, the Comtois became famous as an army horse. Today the Comtois is mainly used for lumbering and work in the vineyards. Louis XIV used the Comtois for his cavalry and artillery. Since the nineteenth century, the Comtois has been mixed with other breeds.

Above: Tarrying time has to be allowed for and is not quite the same as idleness.
Left: Quintal regards the camera with curiosity.
Right: Quintal and Quiri du Crête, with their Swiss owner and his dog.

HEAVY HORSES AT WORK

In the Country

It is rare to see work horses pulling agricultural equipment in today's mechanized world. However, the Amish, a Christian sect in North America, use horses exclusively for work and transportation. Haste and noise are quite alien to them, in striking contrast to life in our modern world. Their rhythm is set by dawn and dusk, by the seasons, the weather and more than anything else, by their serenity.

Today much of the equipment designed for "horse power" is dated and to see it still in use on these farms is quite amazing. With the growing interest in work horses, some manufacturers are now offering machines of modern concept to this limited sector of the farming world.

Top: Cultivating — weeding and loosening the soil between the young corn plants — takes a steady team and a steady mind. This ecologically sound method has unfortunately been replaced by herbicides.
Bottom: When mowing, the "inside horse" often has an obvious advantage. The other horse has no choice but to watch its teammate getting all the tasty morsels.

Top: Harvesting with Shires at Holme upon Spalding Moor in England.
Bottom: Sheaves of grain in an Ohio landscape.
Opposite: Haying season near Millersburg, Ohio.
Overleaf: A farmer and his team-of-four are working down a field of grain.

Top left and opposite: Here the loading of hay is done mechanically by the implement which is towed behind the wagon. The men do the hard work of stowing the hay, while the little girl very gracefully controls the four horses. She has to steer judiciously over the row of raked hay. In the final picture she is still at the reins — hidden away in the hay. Bottom: Time is precious when the clouds are darkening.

Heavy Horses in Town

Town scenery provides a very different milieu. Surprisingly, a few breweries still operate in various parts of the world, making daily deliveries to pubs. They generally use rubber-tired drays pulled by a pair of horses, which are actually quite economical for short hauls within two to three miles and less of a nuisance to present-day traffic than one might expect. Using back streets whenever possible and performing a lively trot in between, they are tolerated by other road users as an exception to the rule, and generally regarded with an amused smile. Belgians are favored among European breweries on the continent.

There is often much waiting time for dray horses — and some diversions as well, such as the attentions paid to them by some pedestrians — perhaps they receive an occasional apple or lump of sugar. Mostly, they have to contend with their own company. Once standing still, most of these horses will stay put, but their driver will often apply a chock or a brake just to make sure. These scenes were captured in Hannover and Munich, West Germany.

Rosa and David

This pair of Belgians, David and Rosa from Hannover, Germany, once made headlines in the newspaper. Without a driver they completed a circumnavigation of the town district following their customary route! Apparently, they did quite well on their own, only slightly damaging one car (which was parked too close to a corner). Because no one told them to stop when they passed the pubs, they kept right on going, making good time getting back to the brewery and their stable.

Horses have very good hearing. One place where this becomes evident is at a traffic light. Being slower than the rest of the traffic, draymen try not to run a yellow light, which means horse-drawn vehicles usually end up in front at the crossing. Some teamsters have noticed that at familiar crossings horses throw their weight into the harness a fraction of a second before the light changes from red to green as though by instinct. The explanation is as simple as most miracles and hardly less amazing: the horses can hear the clicks of the relay switch that operates the lights (which may be located in a box across the street) and have learned to distinguish the sounds that signify the change to green.

Opposite: Monti and Rigo, two Shires, wait patiently.

Below: Rigo and Domingo in Lucerne, Switzerland.
Opposite: This horse has a "moustache" that is a common characteristic among Shires.

In the good old days, the guild of draymen was considered by some a byword of dipsomania. In spite of the drayman's exposure both to the "brew" and the public, his questionable reputation was not to be blamed entirely on thirst, but rather on circumstances. In many cases the driver's excessive drinking was a form of self-defense. On hot summer days when inns kept running out of beverage, a drayman's only "safe" way to be relieved of his duties at the end of a day was to get so intoxicated that he was no longer capable of making another delivery.

Professional drivers, also known as teamsters, carters or draymen, tend to be quite affable and friendly. They love to chat and are eager to impart anecdotes about their teams. Stablemen or hostlers, who are responsible for the daily maintenance of the stables and the horses, are more reticent and protective of their territory. With the advent of unions, regulated working hours and guaranteed wages, today's draymen have a respectable income — which has not always been the case.

Opposite: Draft horses are indifferent to the passing traffic.
Below: After work, Monti and Rigo are led to the stable.

Aladdin and Ali Baba. Many horses with a star on the forehead have been named after the character in the tale, "Aladdin's Lamp."

It is amazing how patiently some dray horses wait while their driver finishes up business. They barely move a step. Once the coachman disappears inside the pub to fulfill orders, all that is left to the "waiters" outside is plenty of time and their apparent faith in the human race. A spectator who wants to catch a dray on the move has to be almost as patient as a horse. Eventually, the driver climbs up to his box and the horses start moving. They will soon be out of sight as their pace is always faster than a person can walk.

Several breweries in Switzerland still use horses for daily deliveries year-round. Special attention to the horse's coat is required during the winter when Belgians grow a thick coat. If the horses were just out in the pasture, nature's overcoat would be fine. However, extended drives at a brisk pace cause the animals to sweat, and such intense activity alternated with long waiting periods when the horses must remain stationary can create health problems for them. To compensate for these extreme conditions, part of the horse's coat is cropped close and the hair on the legs is left long. The horse will dissipate the generated heat more quickly and sweat less. Blankets keep the horse's body warm during waiting periods.

Opposite: Old Barrick just props his head up on the pole when he needs a break. He is the only stallion in his outfit and the oldest; the seven other Belgians are geldings. They work five days a week and have three meals a day (two on weekends). They also have a spacious stable, and hostlers and coachmen to attend to their needs.

Breweries in Continental Europe favor Belgians. Some Belgians have their tails "docked." When they are young, part of the tail as well as the hair is cut off. It is questionable where this practice originated. Many cosmetic changes inflicted on animals were initiated out of practicality; in the case of docking, it was perhaps to prevent the horse's tail from becoming entangled in the reins. Some people think that the muscle power of a team of heavy horses is more apparent when their tails are docked. It adds a rather denuded quality to their appearance. Today the practice is illegal in many countries. Docking deprives the horse of its most efficient defense against flies and other insects.

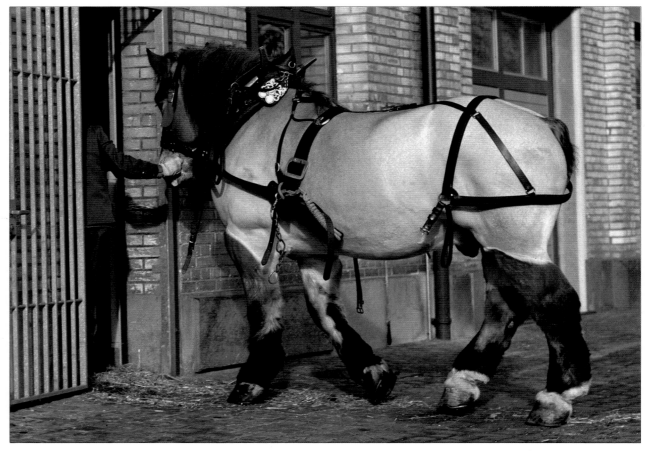

When running free, heavy horses require little grooming, but it is a different story for horses who are working, partly because they sweat more. As a result, increased metabolic waste is eliminated through the skin where it combines with dust from the straw or wood shavings used in the stalls. This dirt is removed with a currycomb. The drivers who groom the horses observe a type of ritual when they discard the dust from the comb onto the floor at regular intervals. The distinctive marks that are left behind (see photograph) are considered a sign of the groom's skill and devotion.

In the past, the apron running along the stalls was swept clean and even wetted prior to grooming so that these marks could be seen better. Needless to say, no one was allowed to "cover one's tracks," and indeed no sweeping was permitted throughout the stables until the equerry or foreman had checked on each teamster's work. The marks were scrutinized and counted as well — twelve decent prints were considered the bare minimum. The exact number is still causing contention among old hands today.

Some people are always looking for an easy way out. Inventive grooms, who are underpaid and overworked, have been known to collect ashes from the hearth and substitute them for the dust in order to meet their quota.

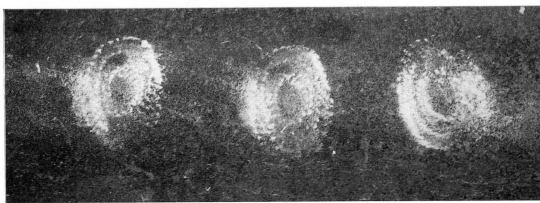

Runic marks on the stable floor.
(see text)

75

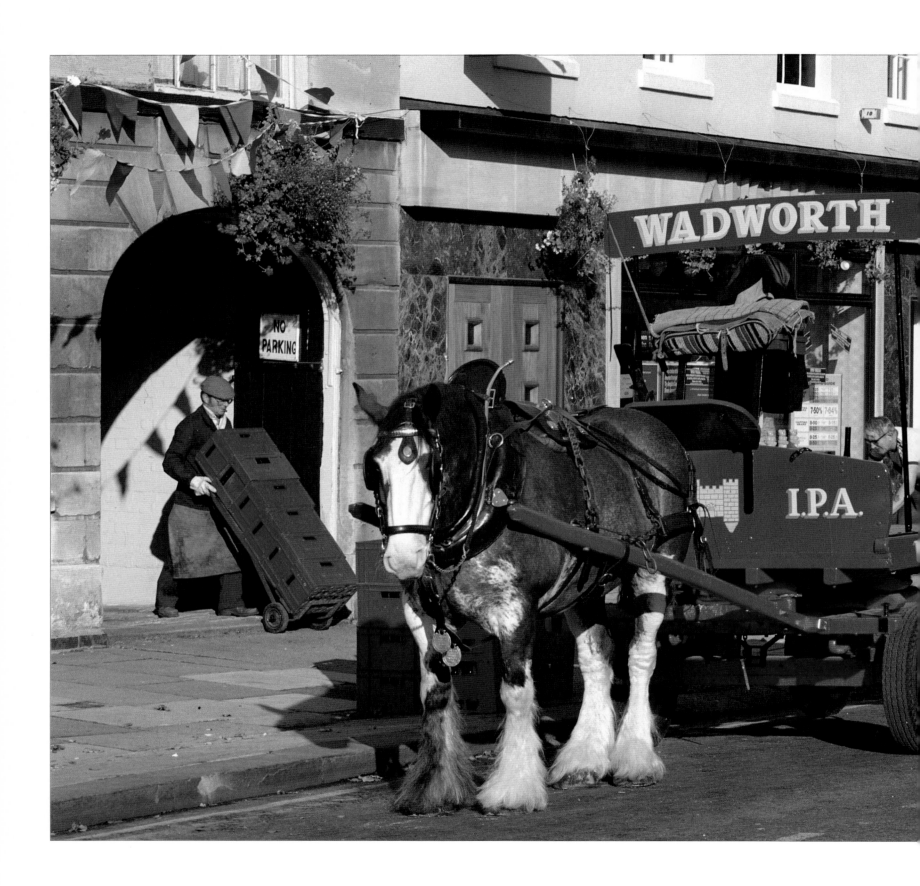

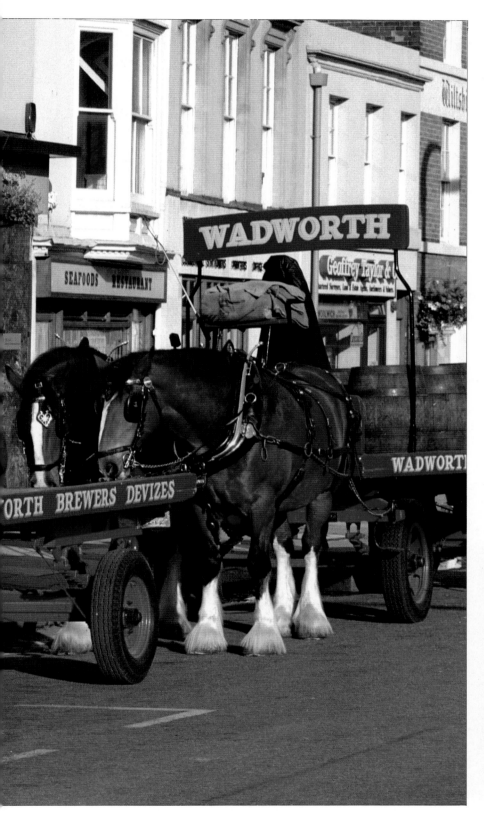

The traditional brewery horse in England is, of course, a Shire.

Fairs and Competitions

Today, when modern traffic has almost eliminated the draft horse from our towns and countryside, public events such as fairs and agricultural shows represent a rare opportunity to see and experience the world of heavy horses, albeit a Sunday world. There one can admire beautiful, well-fed creatures nicely groomed and decorated, sparkling harnesses, immaculate carriages and historic brewery drays — quite different from hard working farm or cart horses with their worn and faded gear, or even the brewery teams on a daily delivery routine.

Horse shows with classes for heavy horses are almost as old as some of the horse breeds themselves. Very early shows did not have separate classes for the various breeds, nor was the practice of awarding prizes always as popular as it is today. When first proposed at a Suffolk show in England, none of the participants seemed to be ready to accept anything but first prize for their entry and the discriminating idea was postponed for some time.

The highlight of any horse show is when the driving performance of "turn-outs," or horse-drawn carriages, is judged. Horse, harness and carriage are inspected as well.

A handsome brewery team at the fairgrounds of an English country town. Nowadays few could afford the expenditure of time and money required for such a lavish display.

Horses' decorations can be as simple as ribbons and plaiting or as elaborate as ear coverings and medallions. Braiding the mane and tail of a horse is an important part of its decoration, requiring skill and patience on the part of both parties to get it all in place. Braiding styles vary not only from country to country but also among breeds. Sometimes styles are related to function, depending on whether a horse is hitched to a wagon or presented "in hand."

Opposite and above: Typical Bavarian "Kaltblut" (cold-blood) horses: blond manes against a bay, almost dun body.
Below: A breed from northern Germany called Schleswiger.

An event at the British National Ploughing Competition at Bridge Sollers, 1986.

Plowing competitions are the liveliest events in which heavy horses participate and are usually, weather permitting, lots of fun for the contestants. Though the combination of pride and concentration are bound to make some plowmen sweat, the general gusto turns work into play. Watching others work has always been a great pastime, too.

A plowing match may involve no more than a handful of farmers and teams from the surrounding area and an audience of relatives, friends and a few passing strangers. It may involve a commercial organization that has teams arriving from far and wide in a fleet of horsetrailers, with an expectant multitude looking on.

It is difficult to explain to the layman all the intricacies involved in a plowing competition. The classic plow for most of us is the one where the plowman walks behind, steering manually with a pair of handles. Typically, there are two iron wheels in front of the share which look rather awkwardly matched: the larger one runs in the furrow and the smaller one on the field. Similarly, the two horses used for plowing have a somewhat unequal job, although they are matched in size. The left-hand one is always the "field horse" while the right-hand one walks the furrow as neatly as a tightrope dancer. The reason for such inveterate division of labor is due to the share, which is rigidly fixed (unlike the reversible plows of more modern equipment). The fixed plow can only throw the furrow to the right side, which means the farmer must alternate rows and is not able to make the return trip along the same furrow. A special system of plowing has been created to ensure that all furrows join evenly, following the same pattern.

To confuse matters further, half of the plot is to be plowed clockwise, the other half counterclockwise. The turning is done on the "headlands" with the plowshare above the ground.

The various types of horse-drawn plows are fascinating examples of human ingenuity and require expertise from the plowmen who use them. At frequent intervals, the contestant exchanges the reins for a wrench, adjusting some nuts and bolts, a task often quite difficult because the plow has been freshly painted for the occasion.

Today, when practically all plowing is done by tractor, farmers (even if they are horse enthusiasts), rarely have time to practice for competitions. This is more apparent with the horses; after the crucial first furrows or "the opening" is plowed, the plowman will often have a helper in front (walking backwards) to guide the horses along. Alas, it costs minus points, but not as many as badly-run furrows do. After several passages up and down the field, most teams get the hang of it.

*British National Ploughing
Competition at Bridge Sollers.*

American Belgians plowing. The reversible plow used here often requires larger teams.
Overleaf: A plowing match in upstate New York.

Left: Bavarian "Festzug" in Munich where horses and their drivers are dressed in ornamental costumes. The barrels, alas, are ornamental too. The full ones are delivered by truck without much ado. These horses are European Belgians.

Below: Organic horsepower juxtaposed next to an oil company's logo.

Originally, teams-of-four or more were essential for pulling the heavy drays over steep hills. Today, multiple teams are used primarily for aesthetic purposes.

Above: A team-of-four Shire geldings in Lucerne, Switzerland.
Right: A publicity drive with a brief stop.

A favorite pastime for horses in general (and draft horses in particular) is to get hold of anything they can reach with their mouth and investigate it by pulling or chewing. In order to avoid damage to the gear, much of the harness and gear in front is covered with metal or made from it. In some countries the problem is dealt with at its source: a metal basket is attached to the bridle covering the horse's mouth.

Top: Jousting knights "feeling their oats."
Bottom: Lunchtime break.

Left: This container looks like it was dropped from Outer Space. The "sighting" was somewhere near Frankenland, West Germany. These transport boxes have spindle-geared legs in each corner which means the box can be swiftly raised to the necessary height in order for a horse-trailer to drive underneath for pick-up. It greatly facilitates loading and unloading heavy horses but is still somewhat slower than using a ramp. Below and opposite: Preparing a team-of-six for a parade. The horses will patiently endure whatever is bestowed upon them.

101

Above: Nothing beats a bite of greens!
Below: The best method of judging a horse's age.
Opposite above: The center of a ten-horse team.
Opposite below: A team-of-six on its way to a display in a little township in Germany.

Horses in banking center, Zurich.

BREEDING AND REARING

Above: Stypewood Grange, a gorgeous stud farm near Hungerford in Berkshire; a grey Shire mare in the foreground.
Right and opposite: A magnificent Clydesdale stallion. Although advanced in years, his power is still impressive. Shewalton Lodge, Ayrshire, Scotland.

In Normandy, among the hills of Merlerault, stands the Haras du Pin, a castle that includes a royal stud farm, decreed under Louis XIV and completed in 1730. Today it is one of the few remaining government studs for Percheron horses in France. Parts of the buildings house offices, tack rooms and many spacious stables. Most of the stables are reserved for warm-blooded stud horses and riding stock.

There are approximately twenty Percheron stallions at the Haras du Pin. The majority of them spend the months from January to July at outlying stations, where they stand stud for the benefit of local breeders or farmers who save the time and cost of long-distance transportation of their mares. Stud fees are supposed to be nominal. Soon after the stallions return in July, the entire horse stock of the Haras is presented to the director for inspection. Each horse's state of health is closely examined and compared to its previous record.

Below: The standard breed offers a striking comparison to the heavy breed.
Bottom: Official inspection by the director of the Haras early in the morning when everything is still veiled in mist.

Percheron stallions are often hitched up together. This is not the case with other breeds, as they tend to be unpredictable or aggressive toward a team-mate, seeing him as a potential rival. But today the chances of encountering a flirtatious mare en route are slim. Traffic jams are more likely and much less of a challenge. Incidentally, coachmen never seem to stray far from their parked horses.

Above: A hay wagon is pulled by a frisky team.
Opposite: Carting various goods between barns and stables.

Sometimes it is more practical for workhorses to be kept in stables when they are not working rather than out in the pasture. The horses shown here are stallions and if turned out, each would probably need a pasture of his own, not bordering his neighbor's.

Percherons are born black. Some of them stay that color, but most soon develop dapples on their coat, with black freckles remaining around the mouth and nose for some time. The mature horse may end up perfectly white, but the dappled grey is more common.

Opposite: The inside passageway of one of the barns at Haras du Pin.

Stud Service

At a time when people are becoming increasingly suspicious of man's interference with nature, looking at the development of heavy horses as a positive example of such "meddling" may provide some comfort. The natural beauty manifested in a Percheron or Shire, or one of the other "heavies," is the result of selective breeding rather than evolution. These horses' proverbial friendliness and quiet temper are also achievements of such breeding.

Left: The leather straps being carried here will be needed later on. Since the hooves of many brood mares working on farms are shod, their metal is potentially dangerous to an amorous stallion. The straps are used to limit the movement of a whimsical or jumpy mare should she suddenly decide to kick.

This mare refuses the stallion, a positive indication that the stallion's previous visit some days earlier was a success. Usually, to avoid any risk, a stallion is taken to a mare more than once so that the owner doesn't have to chance another year's wait for a foal. The mare's fury is restrained by the use of leather straps.

Below: The "tender returns" of last year's engagement; after its father's departure, a little colt rejoins the now relaxed mother and their proud owner.

Anyone who has witnessed the casual, unforeseen encounter between a mare in heat and a stallion "in the wrong place" will probably not forget the experience, particularly if he happens to be holding the reins of one of them. Presence of mind will usually succeed in bringing things under control. Yet after the tempest of ardent passion has subsided, one cannot help but muse upon the magnificent spectacle that could have unrolled under more natural circumstances. As far as the practice of heavy horse breeding is concerned, the sad part of the story is that in reality circumstances are more prosaic than congenial. Most breeding procedures provide neither the time nor adequate space to allow for the normal mating ritual common among horses.

Of course there are many practical and economic reasons for this state of affairs; it has always been that way. It seems to be the price one has to pay.

This page and opposite: In spite of his fiery stride, Paolo is a particularly good-natured stallion according to his warden. Some stallions' stamina and unrelenting excitement are quite amazing. Even with ready and willing partners, constant lack of time distorts an event that is graceful by nature.

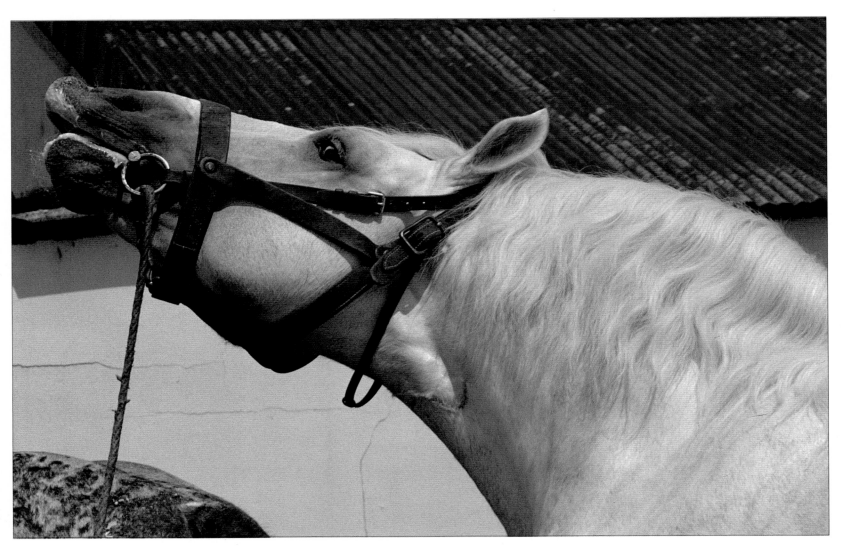

This curious behavior, when the horse flips its upper lip over the nostrils, baring the front teeth, and rolls its eyes while holding its slightly swaying head raised up, definitely has some primeval, almost demonic, look! This pose, when displayed by a powerful stallion, can be quite menacing to someone confronting it for the first time. Spectators, standing safely behind a fence, are more likely to be embarrassed by such strange manners.

The horse's behavior is prompted by certain smells. Unlike the cock's crowing on a dung-hill, a horse's posture when turning up its nose is an internal matter; by curling its lip upwards over its nostrils the horse effectively closes off the air inside the nose cavity. This allows the animal to analyze a particular scent that interests it, without "outside interference." Even newborn foals can be seen "putting on the style" when they are tickled by a strange smell.

The stallion, a Shire, is very much aware of the two mares in the background and the pose he assumes leaves no doubt about his territorial claim.

Top: Two Percheron families in the United States.
Opposite above: Percheron mare with her foal;
Holmes County, Ohio.
Opposite below: Mother and child. Foals usually
come in singles; twins are rare and often too
delicate to survive.

Mares and Foals

Above: These two youngsters have obviously found a useful tree.
Opposite above: Mates — pugnacious ones that is!
Opposite below: At the end of their animated discussion a halter was missing.

Pastures and Pastimes

Stallions cannot be kept together in the same pasture, for they will immediately start fighting ferociously. The fights between these geldings, mostly a game, are quite harmless. Some scars suggest that they may play rough at times. Most injuries, however, can be blamed on the horses' iron shoes, fences or other objects foreign to their natural environment.

Top: These geldings belonging to a Frankfurt brewery work only one day a week or so. The rest of the time they reside on a farm which is also host to a riding school. Their lot in life has certainly improved when compared with the rigorous work loads of past generations of draft horses.

Bottom: It is entertaining to observe how horses interact with one another. Sometimes they challenge each other, but they also seem willing to put their animosities aside and help each other out. It is common to see horses plucking each other's back and withers when they lose their thick winter coat in the springtime. Rolling in the grass is also a favorite pastime.

Breaking-In

The training of young horses, a procedure called "breaking-in," is much easier when an experienced horse is hitched alongside the beginner. A sled, which allows the driver to sit rather than having to walk alongside, is used for pulling. The extra weight accustoms the horse to the pressure of the harness against its body. The sled was sometimes called a stoneboat, which describes the type of ballast that was often applied, as well as the kind of ride one was likely to get if one got off-course.

A training exercise using a "stoneboat" in the Ohio countryside.

FARRIERY

There was a time (some may still remember) when nothing was quite as exciting for a youngster as being allowed to watch the farrier at work: shoeing horses at the blacksmith's shop with its miraculous forge and bellows, devil tongs and sizzling water! The cheerful din of regular hammer blows and alternate tapping gradually changed from a clank to a ring as the heated iron cooled off and hardened. And who could forget the amazing spectacle of iron drawn from the blaze of a forge, the brilliant white-yellow light turning slowly to red under flying cinders, then covering itself with a uniform grey that concealed its ferocious heat, and finally the metal being placed aside so that no one could stumble on it.

Farriers still exist in some areas, straddling past and present. Today, prefabricated horseshoes come in various shapes and sizes, nailholes included, but the irons must still be heated and shaped to each horse's needs. Although it isn't necessary to shoe all horses, shoeing is essential once they are used for regular work, especially on hard surfaces. Since the horses' hooves keep growing, the irons have to be changed about every six weeks, to trim the horn as well as to replace worn shoes.

Despite their considerable bulk, heavy horses are not more difficult to shoe, for their quiet disposition and cooperation make up for the added weight. The farrier starts with the forefeet first; since horses are very curious by nature, they feel more at ease if they can see what is going on. Besides, a horse supports most of its weight on the front legs and does not like to hold one of them up for long. By the time the horse's patience is wearing thin, the hind legs are ready to be shoed, an easier task as horses are used to shifting back weight. They can often be seen with a hind foot cocked when relaxing.

Left: Sometimes sturdy racks are used to support and restrict horses while they are being shod. The horse in the photo looks a little disgruntled.

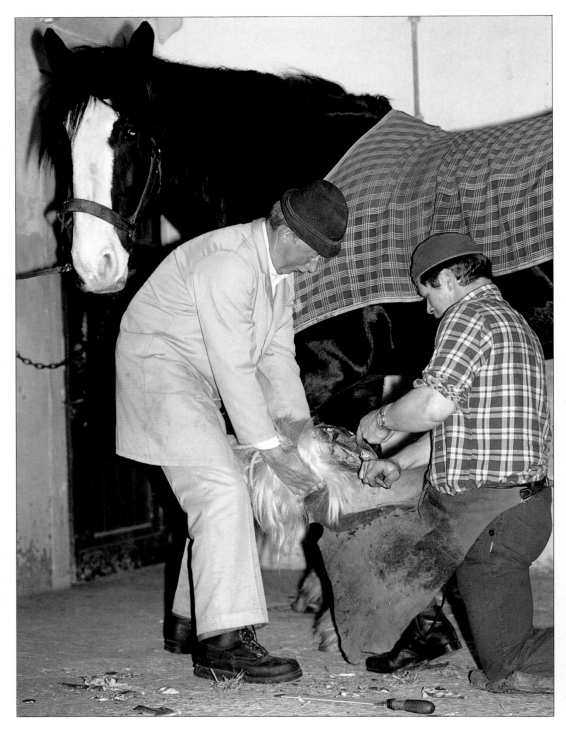

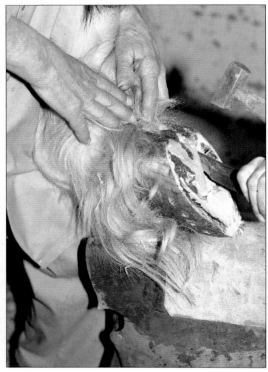

Above: Trimming the hoof's horn after taking off the used iron.
Opposite far right: The horses are usually unconcerned about the hissing smoke; they don't feel the heat and don't mind the smell, but do seem to wonder where it comes from. The marks left by the heated iron will tell the farrier whether the shoe is fitting well or needs to be better shaped.
Opposite right: The point of the last nail is still visible where it came through

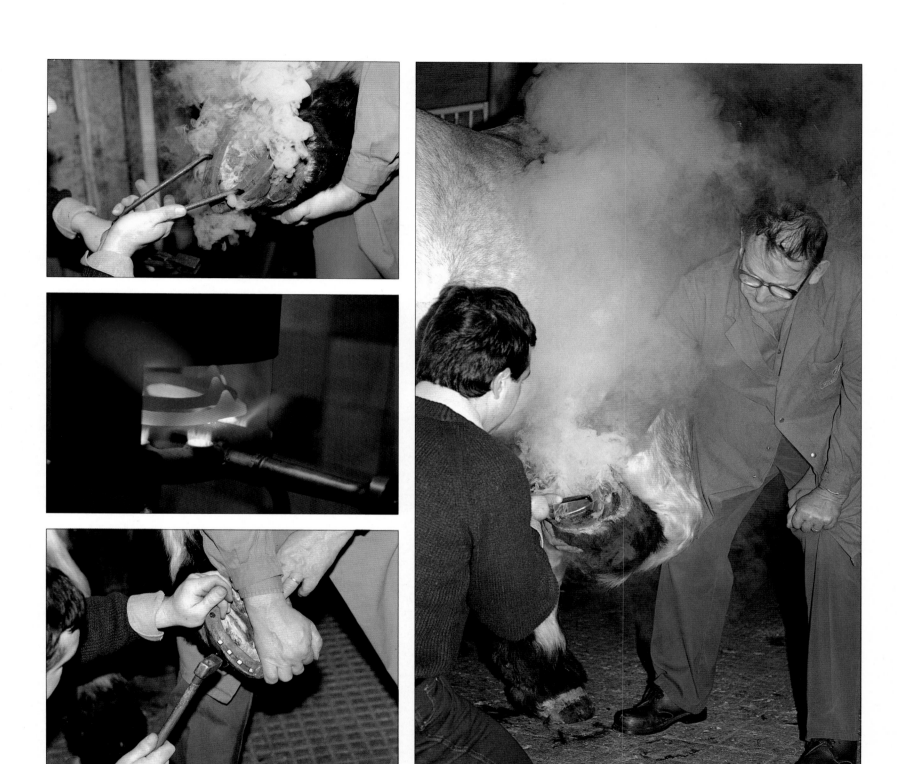

the hoof. The excess will be cut off and the end clenched flat. Driving a
nail into a horse's hoof and knowing where it will come out takes skill and
practice; there isn't much leeway for error as lameness can be the conse-
quence. The hole at the horn of the iron is threaded to receive the "calk," a
removable stud that prevents the horse from skidding on slippery or icy
road surfaces.

IMPRESSIONS

The Amish

Branching off a modern highway somewhere near Millersburg, Ohio, the traveler suddenly finds himself in a different world, although the change comes almost imperceptibly. One notices first that the road markings on the surface and along the sides have disappeared. The difference is even more obvious at night. After turning off the car lights, the surrounding darkness is complete; there are no street lights. This is the country of the Amish.

Of course it was not by chance that I had driven here, for I was now in horse country! I soon realized that the primary means of transportation here is the buggy. The area is also a haven for heavy horses. During the day, they can be seen grazing in pastures and engaged in work in the fields. This area is unique because it is one of the few places left in the Western world where one can see heavy horses at work on a daily basis, except on Sundays.

The Amish have no churches and keep their service every two weeks in alternate barns on the various farms (the barns are usually built by the entire community's work force, sometimes in a single day). Each parish comprises barely a dozen families, headed by a bishop; on the second Sunday they visit with neighboring parishes.

The Amish are members of the Christian faith but follow their own interpretation of it. Their belief incorporates many stringent rules relating to practical life. The result is not always practical, but meaningful for the Amish. Their sole use of horses, in a country that has all but abandoned animals as a means of transport or work, stems from their ban on cars and tractors. Their houses have no electricity or telephones and the countryside is devoid of transmission-lines — not even a telephone post is visible.

Though the uncluttered skies may solve some background problems for the photographer, the real challenge waits for him in the "foreground." Most of the Amish farmers do not mind having their horses photographed, but they do object to being photographed themselves. The Amish have a strong aversion to all forms of vanity; one of the last things they want is to appear to be posing for a picture. The rare occasion when, despite all efforts, I captured a driver at the end of the reins, can be blamed on the horses that dragged him into the picture. To put it more justly, I photographed the horses at an angle or distance that respected Amish reservations. Eventually, I did have to return to a different world, one that seems to have lost much of the charm of that magic place where people always have time for a talk and an abiding respect for horses!

Sugaring in Vermont

In New England, workhorses have a very special job during a two-to-three-week period each year, the maple syrup harvest. Some farmers keep a team of horses for the sole purpose of having them on hand when "sugaring" takes place, usually in March. The famous syrup is obtained from the sap of maple trees. The watery sap drips into buckets which have to be emptied once a day or so, usually into the tank of some horse-drawn vehicle. Horses are ideally suited for this job because the woods where the maples grow, called a "sugar bush," are often in hilly country with dirt roads. What makes matters worse is that the sap flows during the last days of winter, a time of snow and mud. Only when it still freezes at night but warms up in daytime will those buckets start to fill. Depending on conditions, the tank is carried on a sleigh or a sled with wheels in front. After doing a round of the sugar bush, the loaded cart is hauled to a small structure in the forest where the tank is emptied. As the team starts out for another trip, the sap is immediately boiled down to syrup inside the sugarhouse. A terrific fire is kept up; the long stacks of wood outside offer more than a hint of the stoker's determination.

For the horses the going is often quite rough. It takes a disciplined animal that is willing to give all its power when needed and yet is able to stand still on command wherever it may be, even if in an awkward place such as an icy-cold ditch, or just beyond reach of a hemlock twig!

Some teams are surrounded by yelling and others by the ringing of bells; both are aids in finding them in the maze of trails and trees. Long before coming upon those sounds, the traveler will notice something else from afar, even if the sugarhouse with its cupola is still hidden from view: a mighty waft of steam rising slowly from amongst some trees and drifting above the grey hills. It will certainly not be the only one that day in the Green Mountains, and maybe not even that night, when the sparks will be telling the tale.

Right and below: Prince and Andy, a team from Canada. A beautiful example of a Belgian-Percheron mix. Opposite: A team of American Belgians.

Sleigh Rides

Bob Gove's sleigh rides are not only an excursion into Vermont's countryside, but also provide an opportunity to relive a moment from the past. Bob stops his team at frequent intervals, especially when driving through deep snow, as the horses are no longer accustomed to regular work and tire quickly. He turns around to his passengers to explain what goes on in the country, and eventually launches into yet another of his stories. Everyone seems to thrive on them, including the resting horses.

Logging

Horse people often impart stories about their favorite horses. One farmer in Vermont told me about his American-bred Belgian, Mark. This unique stallion was not only trained in skidding logs but also in the art of getting on board the transport trucks — without the assistance of a ramp!

Once harnessed, Mark would scan the yard, and head straight for any truck that had a lowered tailgate. He would rear back on his hind legs and jump on, clearing any cargo or logging equipment already there.

But how did he get down? Backwards! Once the tailgate was lowered and Mark was commanded to come out, he would move cautiously toward the back of the truck and stretch a hind leg into midair, waving it exploringly. Suddenly, he would execute a wild backwards leap, harness chains ringing, and land firmly on the ground with a snort. Visitors to the farm were advised to keep their tailgates shut, just in case.

Weekend exercise, Zurich, Switzerland.

Acknowledgments

I would like to thank Laura Lee, Dana Jinkins and Jill Bobrow for their encouragement as well as for their contributions to this book. Without them, this would not have been realized. I would also like to thank Janet, Bonnie, Cheryl and Bob for their invaluable assistance.

I want to thank Chronicle Books for trusting that this type of book was not so esoteric after all.

Special thanks to the many friendly helpers and hard workers along the road — to the farmers, the teamsters, the drivers and foremen of my "favorite" breweries and the hospitable Amish parish which put me up — and all those who managed to put up with me.

I would also like to thank my Aunt Dorothea Siemsen for her loving support of this book since its inception. And a thank-you to Kenny and Dana for their patronage and for sharing their lovely Vermont farm with me.

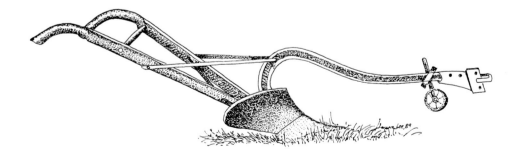